Fairly Grim Tales

BEDTIME STORIES
for the
RICH and/or FAMOUS

 as told by
L.K. PETERSON

illustrated by
TOM HACHTMAN

For Deborah

Disclaimer

Nobody rich and/or famous was harmed during the making of this book.

Cover illustrations by Tom Hachtman
Book layout by Martin Kozlowski

For more on Now What Media Books,
please visit nowwhatmedia.com/nowwhatbooks.html

Table O' Contents

Goldilocks & The Three Tenors

GOLDILOCKS (she went by just one name) lived high on a hill, in a cantilevered castle that had the very best view of the Woodland.

For her birthday her mother and her mother's new husband told Goldilocks that she could have anything she wanted.

"Meh!" whined Goldilocks, "That's what I *always* get!"

What Goldilocks wanted this year, she told them, was to have the most fabulously spectacular birthday party ever; something like nothing she or any of her friends had ever had before.

Specifically, Goldilocks said, she wanted a very loud tenor to sing at her party. Now, Goldilocks didn't know much about tenors, but she did know that no one she knew had ever had one sing at *their* birthday party.

Mother's new husband, who had connections in the music business, commissioned a cantata for the occasion but Goldilocks insisted on casting the tenor herself.

She had her people put an ad in *Daily Variety* and on craigslist.

"*Wanted . . .*"

the ad read,

"*. . . very loud tenor to sing at fabulously spectacular birthday party. Must bring down the house!*"

On the day of the auditions, a line of tenors wound around the castle grounds and zigzagged halfway down the hill.

One after another the tenors came in, belted out an aria and left their head shots.

And one after another Goldilocks told them, "Thank you. *Next!*"

By late afternoon, there were only three left.

"Hmmm," said Goldilocks, looking over the trio, "This one's too fat. He'll eat all the foie gras. That one just hasn't got, I don't know, *je ne sais quois*. And that guy," she said, squinting at the third tenor, who was holding a leaf-blower, "Looks a lot like the gardener."

No, none of them was quite right.

Suddenly, Goldilocks got an idea. She had all three tenors stand close together and told them to sing the same note as loudly as they could, all at the same time, and to hold it for as long as they could.

And on her cue . . .

"Okay, boys! Hit it!"

. . . they did.

As the trio boomed and bellowed, the
chandeliers shivered, the tiles trembled
and the walls wobbled. The whole castle
quaked and there came a thunderous roar
from under the floor.

The castle rocked this way and that, then
toppled over and crashed down the hill
into the valley below, leaving a terrible
mess and tying up cross-town traffic
something awful.

Sure enough, the three tenors had brought
down the house.

With the castle now at the bottom of the
hill, Goldilocks had her birthday party in

a public park, catered by a dented-up food truck that smelled funny and was usually parked by the bus depot, which while not fabulously spectacular, was something that she and her friends had never done before.

Moral: *People who live in cantilevered castles shouldn't cast cantatas.*

Mr. Toad's Last Ride

MR. Toad lived on the cushiest lily pad in the Woodlands' pond.

From where he sat, there were always plenty of flies, bugs and insects within easy tongue-flicking range; he hardly had to do anything to get them. As lily pads in ponds go, this was prime real estate and everyone knew how lucky Mr. Toad was to have it.

Except Mr. Toad.

After several seasons there, Mr. Toad decided that it wasn't his lily pad's location that attracted the flies, bugs and insects, it was *him*.

"I don't have to stay here," Mr. Toad thought," they'll come to wherever I am!"

And with that, Mr. Toad leapt off his lily pad and hopped away.

The other amphibians in the pond were so astonished that it was nearly two-and-a-half minutes before they started fighting over who'd get the prime lily pad next.

Meanwhile, as Mr. Toad went hopping around the Woodland, his blood sugar level dropped and dropped.

"Where are all those stupid flies, bugs and insects?" Mr. Toad wondered, "Don't they know I'm hungry?"

Mr. Toad started flicking his sticky tongue at every creature he came across none of whom, it turned out, cared to be eaten by him.

"Hey, cut that out!" said a mole Mr. Toad had flicked his tongue at, "I'm not an insect!"

"Don't you know who I am?" demanded Mr. Toad.

"Yeah," replied the mole, "You're that crazy-ass toad who left the best lily pad in the pond."

"That's MISTER Crazy Ass Toad, to you!" bellowed Mr. Toad, "Be my lunch!"

"Yeah, whatever," replied the mole as he turned away and went back to whatever it is moles do.

"He was too small, anyway," snorted Mr. Toad as he hopped away, "I deserve bigger."

All afternoon, as Mr. Toad went around flicking his tongue at various creatures who didn't want to be his food, he'd noticed large flying insects in the sky high above, going past regularly and always in the same direction.

"Hmmm," he thought, "Maybe I should

stick to flicking my tongue at things with wings. If I can get close enough, I bet I can catch one of those."

Mr. Toad hopped his way up the highest hill over the Woodland where, every few minutes, one of these huge — and very noisy — flying insects would whoosh overhead. But, even from this highest ground, his tongue couldn't reach them.

So Mr. Toad hopped to the top of the "D" of the Woodland sign and waited. As the next giant flying insect approached, Mr. Toad leapt up toward it as high as he could, flicked his tongue out farther than he had ever flicked it before and, sure enough, he made contact!

Mr. Toad was last seen zooming off into the wild blue yonder, his tongue stuck like glue to Delta's 7:10 flight to Cincinnati, flapping along behind it like the tail of a kite.

Although his body was never found, Woodland authorities eventually pronounced Mr. Toad "missing and presumed croaked."

Moral: *Having it too easy is getting harder all the time.*

The Surfer's Fish Tale

ONCE UPON A TIME a surfer who'd
paddled far offshore from the Woodland's
beach sat waiting to catch a wave.

Suddenly, a fish jumped out of the water
and landed on his board.

The surfer stared down at the fish in
astonishment and the fish, equally
astonished, stared back up at the surfer.

Finally, the fish spoke up.

"A little help, here?"

"A talking fish!" said the surfer, now really astonished.

"Not for long if you don't get me back into the water," said the fish.

The surfer was about to pick up the fish and toss him back when he hesitated and asked, "Wait, what's in it for me?"

"I dunno, there's the whole 'saving my life' thing. . ." the fish said.

"Well, since you can talk, you must be some kind of magic fish, or something," said the surfer, "Grant me three wishes and I'll put you back in the water.."

"Three wishes? I'm a fish, not a genie!" replied the fish, "One wish, take it or leave it."

"Okay," said the surfer, "Make me the most famous surfer in these waters."

"Sure, why not," replied the fish.

"When?"

"Eh, soon, I guess."

"Whatever," said the surfer as he swatted the fish from his board and back into the sea.

Once safely beneath the waves, the fish, who had no power to grant any number of wishes and had just said that to get back into the water, told his friends about the surfer just above them he'd promised

to make famous. They all had a good laugh about it and told their friends who then told their friends and before long fish from all over had gathered for a look at this gullible surfer.

Just as the surfer was imagining all the sweet endorsement deals that would be coming his way, some pelicans flying by noticed the boatloads of fish clustered around him and commenced dive-bombing them, gobbling up fish by the beak full.

This broke up the crowd pretty quickly and sent the startled surfer paddling back to shore like crazy. Still, for a while there — at least among the fish in it — he was the most famous surfer in those waters.

Moral: *Pelicans are dicks.*

PinocchiCo

ONCE UPON A TIME in the Woodland there was a corporation named PinocchiCo.

As corporations go, PinocchiCo wasn't anything special. Sure it had its fair share of EPA violations, class-action lawsuits, downsizing, outsourcing, unsafe product recalls, hostile takeovers, shady accounting deals and accusations of influence peddling; what made PinocchiCo stand out from the rest was that PinocchiCo wanted to be a *person*.

No corporation had ever become a person before (this was a while back) but PinocchiCo bravely set out to do just that. As it turned out it wasn't really all that difficult and, after greasing a few palms at city hall, PinocchiCo got its wish and was transformed.

And from the first moment PinocchiCo became a person. . . he behaved pretty much the same way as before: he spit his gum out on the sidewalk, jumped into cabs that had stopped for little old ladies, used the "10 Items or Less" checkout line when he had way more than 10 items, talked on his cellphone during movies and bribed his way into trendy restaurants and out of speeding tickets.

Worse yet, every time his bills came due, he'd scream and cry and throw a tantrum, yowling that if he was forced to actually pay up, he'd have to lay off his chauffeur, cook, gardener, housekeeper, sommelier, masseuse and/or personal trainer, then he'd threaten to move away to someplace else and never come back.

This routine worked for longer than you'd like to think, usually netting PinocchiCo a sizeable tax break, despite the fact that the more he lied about his bottom line, the more visibly it grew.

Finally fed up, some concerned citizens united into an angry mob and staged an "intervention" with PinocchiCo.

PinocchiCo just laughed at them, "I never said anything about being a *good* person," he snorted, "Besides, all I have to do is change my name and logo, and I'm back, baby!"

Hearing this — and knowing it was true — the angry mob rushed PinocchiCo, tore his assets to pieces and sold them off at a tidy profit.

Moral: *Corporations are not people, my friend, and if they were, you wouldn't want one sitting behind you at the movies.*

The Beautiful Swan & The Silly Goose

IN THE POND at the center of the Woodland lived a flock of beautiful swans.

One of these swans, however, was so much more beautiful than the others that creatures came from all over just to watch her glide gracefully across the water.

The other swans were terribly jealous of the extra attention she got.

"Hmph!" said one, "Everyone says they like the way she glides, but they're just watching her because of her looks!"

"That's right," said another, "I've seen ducks and geese every bit as graceful as her but you don't see anyone lining up to watch them!"

"Well, you know," said the third, "I have it on good authority that she doesn't even do her own gliding."

The especially beautiful swan overheard this and was very hurt. She knew she was beautiful (she'd seen her reflection) but truly believed that her gliding was as graceful as gliding got and that her looks had nothing to do with it. And she had never, ever used a gliding double.

She decided that to find out once and for all she would have to go undercover as some other type of waterfowl.

To research her ruse, she took several lunch meetings with a duck and lived with a family of geese for a week.

When the beautiful swan returned to the pond, she was cleverly disguised as the silliest goose you ever saw.

She spent the day gracefully gliding back and forth across the pond, all the while keeping a sharp eye out to see if anyone was watching.

Some Woodland creatures standing on the shore — not so many as usual, but respectable for an opening weekend — commented that the silly goose out there sure could glide gracefully.

Even the swans, who normally didn't give geese a second glance, noticed her.

"She does glide well, said one, "I'll give her that."

"Pity she's not a swan," said another, "Then she'd really have something."

"Yes," said the third, "It isn't fair, I suppose, but a goose that silly looking

doesn't stand a chance of succeeding in this pond."

Upon hearing that last remark, the beautiful swan threw off the disguise, revealing herself to be one of them, albeit way more beautiful.

The other swans honked wildly, first in shock and surprise, then with praise for her remarkable performance.

"A tour-de-force!" said one, "If you watch only one swan pretending to be a goose this year, make it her!"

"How brave of you, darling" said another, "What was it like to not be so beautiful?"

"Whose feathers are you wearing?" asked the third, "They are just fabulous!"

The beautiful swan told the others all about how it felt to not be recognized, how many hours it had taken to put on the disguise and how the whole experience had given her a newfound respect for geese and, to a lesser extent, ducks.

As soon as the beautiful swan glided away, once again feeling very good about herself, the other swans started in with the trash talk.

"What a show-off!" said one, "What, exactly, was that supposed to prove?"

"Why would a swan pretend to be a goose?" said another, "Geese want to be swans, not the other way around!"

"Some birds will do anything to get attention," said the third, "Talk about needy!"

Moral: *Birds of a feather, my ass.*

The Entrepreneur's New Gizmo

or

Invisible is the New Black

IN AN ORCHARD at the edge of
the Woodland lived an entrepreneur.
Whenever this entrepreneur introduced a
new gizmo, everyone who was anybody

in the Woodland (which, of course, was everybody), had to have one, even if they didn't know what it did or if it was pretty much the same as the previous gizmo only a little smaller and a different designer color.

One day the entrepreneur went into his workshop and ordered his two tinkerers to come up with a new gizmo.

"Make it smaller than that last one!" he hollered, "And a new color! And I want it by tomorrow!"

When he'd gone, the tinkerers looked at each other in disbelief.

"Smaller?!" said the first tinkerer, "If we made one any smaller you couldn't see it!"

"Well, if it's invisible," said the other, " At least we don't have to come up with a new color for it!"

The tinkerers laughed then, realizing they'd both had the same idea, got to work.

When the entrepreneur came in the next morning, the tinkerers were waiting for him.

"All right," he growled, "What've you got for me?"

The first tinkerer thrust out his hand, palm up, as if holding something, and said proudly, "The New Gizmo!"

The entrepreneur looked down at the tinkerer's empty hand, but before he could say anything, the other tinkerer held out his hand and asked, "Maybe you like this color better?"

The entrepreneur squinted at the first tinkerer's hand, then the other's, then back again.

"I, can't quite, uh..." he stammered.

"Choose between them?" interrupted the first tinkerer. "I know, they're both such amazing colors."

"And you don't have to decide," said the other, "It becomes any color you want it to be!"

"That's because this gizmo works from your own brainpower!" said the first tinkerer, "The higher your I.Q., the more it does!"

"That's right," said the other, "You have to be really smart just to be see this thing!"

"I see," said the entrepreneur, even though he didn't.

He said he saw it because these two tinkerers had produced some pretty amazing gizmos that had made the entrepreneur serious piles of cash, so if they said they'd created a gizmo you had to be smart to see, they probably had but he was too smart to admit that they were smarter than him.

"You've really outdone yourself this time!" said the first tinkerer.

"Eh, yes, so I have," muttered the

entrepreneur, asking, "What does this one do?"

"Everything the last gizmo did," said the other tinkerer, "Plus anything else you want it to."

When the entrepreneur unveiled the New Gizmo to industry reporters, they gazed at his empty palm blankly for a moment before he exclaimed, "It runs exclusively on brainpower! Only those with above-average intelligence can see it, much less make it work!"

"I see," the reporters said, even though they didn't. Not a one of them was about to speak up and reveal that they might not have above-average intelligence. And none of them did.

So the New Gizmo went on sale and there was great anticipation throughout the Woodland.

Now, usually whenever a new gizmo came out, the minute the Woodland's movers and shakers got one, they took every opportunity — and made up even more — to show it off. This time, however, they began canceling breakfast meetings, lunch meetings, dinner meetings and just staying home altogether rather than risk anyone finding out they couldn't see their New Gizmo.

Moving and shaking in the Woodland came to a standstill.

As it happens, the entrepreneur had a
competitor who lived at the opposite end
of the Woodland, and for every gizmo the

entrepreneur made, this competitor made a gadget very much like it.

The competitor was a very smart guy who, while no slouch in the plus size-ego department, didn't need as much stroking.

A reporter from *Gizmo & Gadget Quarterly* brought him a New Gizmo and asked for his opinion of it.

"I don't see it," he said, because he didn't. "And," the competitor continued, "Not because I'm not smart enough to see it but because there's no "it" to see!" adding, "Honestly, what is wrong with you people?"

Just like that, the buzz around the Woodland went from how fabulous the

New Gizmo was to how it didn't work.

"It was okay at first," everyone was saying now, visibly relieved, "Then it kind of flickered and went all invisible. I'm not even sure where it is half the time!"

When the entrepreneur heard about this he burst into the workshop demanding answers.

"It couldn't be a design flaw," said the first tinkerer.

"It must be a manufacturing defect," said the other.

Once all of the the New Gizmos had been "returned", the entrepreneur snarled at the two tinkerers, "Figure out what went wrong and fix it. Or else!"

The two tinkerers looked at the corner of the workshop where they'd pretended to stack the recalled gizmos and then nervously at each other. They knew if they told the entrepreneur the truth that they'd never tinker in the Woodland again.

Then they had an idea.

When the entrepreneur came in the next morning, the tinkerers were waiting for him.

"All right, what've you got for me?" he growled.

"You won't believe it!" said the first tinkerer.

"Try me," replied the entrepreneur.

"They're gone," said the other, "They've been stolen!"

The entrepreneur's jaw dropped, "Stolen!?" he gasped.

"Yep," replied the first tinkerer, "Every last one of them."

"And the blueprints," said the other, "They're gone, too. We could never make the New Gizmo again without those plans!"

The entrepreneur didn't say anything for what seemed like a long time then he asked, "Any clues?"

"Not a one," said the first tinkerer.

"Whoever pulled this off," said the other, "Was pretty clever."

"I'll say," the entrepreneur responded dryly, as he brushed past the tinkerers on his way to call his claims adjuster.

The robbery was never solved and everyone who'd bought a New Gizmo got a coupon for an upgraded older gizmo in one of several new designer colors.

Every once in a while, a New Gizmo shows up for sale on eBay, but you can tell it's a fake as soon as you see it.

Moral: *You can fool some of the people all of the time, and all of the people some of the time, but if you can trick them into fooling themselves you're really on to something.*

The Pig, The Witch & The Cellphone

ONCE UPON A TIME there was a little pig that lived in the Woodland. But an evil witch (who looked beautiful until you got to know her better) cast a spell that made the little pig rude and thoughtless and caused her to turn off her cell phone and ignore calls she was expecting.

Nearby lived a handsome and talented bear, whose success and shiny fur really ticked-off the evil witch who, despite having shown some early promise, was all but washed up in the Woodland.

The bear bravely went out to rescue the little pig from the witch's spell and straighten her out.

But when the bear tried to tell the little pig that she was under a spell, his fearsome-sounding roar startled nearby Woodland creatures.

The evil witch took advantage of this and sent out nasty, highly paid trolls to tell

everyone about how the bear had roared
so ferociously and how very frightened the
little pig had been.

Soon the whole Woodland had heard about
the angry, roaring bear.

"Roaring is bad," said everyone in the Woodland, "Especially roaring at little pigs."

Of course, the trolls didn't say anything about the spell or the witch, and nobody asked why the bear had roared at the little pig.

The bear was confused, "*Of course* I roar," he said to himself, since no one in the Woodland would talk to him anymore, "I'm a frickin' bear!"

Everyone in the Woodland demanded that he apologize for having roared, which the bear thought was strange since he hadn't roared at them. But he did it anyway, since he had to work there and everything.

He also tried to apologize to the little pig but the evil witch wouldn't let him, and threatened to send out even nastier, more highly paid trolls if he came anywhere near.

Knowing that he couldn't beat both an evil witch's spell and so many lying trolls, the bear lumbered away sadly.

Although the bear generally stayed way over on the other side of the Woodland from then on, whenever he passed by, there would be whispered conversations about him:

"There goes that bear who roared at that little pig."

"A troll told me that he ate her, too."

"No, he just roared."

"Are you sure?"

"Who are you gonna believe, me or some highly paid, lying troll."

"He seemed pretty sure. He said the bear's gay, too."

"You are a complete moron."

Eventually, once she was forgotten in the Woodland, the evil witch's powers diminished and the spell was lifted. The little pig realized how much hurt she'd caused the bear she felt just terrible about it. So she spent several wild years on hard partying, unwise marriages, guest shots on reality shows and in adult videos that went viral.

The witch sent out trolls saying that the little pig's behavior was because the bear had roared at her when she was littler, but the only reaction they got was people asking, "Oh, yeah, that evil witch. Whatever happened to her?"

Moral: *Just answer your cell phone, already.*

The Man With The Gold-Plated Touch

ONCE UPON A TIME (but not all that long ago) there lived a rich man named Midas.

Midas had the Golden Touch.

Well, gold-*plated* touch really, since Midas had amassed his fortune by making stuff from the cheapest material he could find then gold-plating the dickens out of it. Nonetheless, everything he touched became very, very shiny.

One day, Midas decided to gold plate the dickens out of a boat.

He hired boat builders to build the biggest, most luxurious-looking boat anyone had ever seen (but to use only the crappiest material), then to gold plate every nautical inch of the thing, stem to stern, crow's nest to keel. And to lay it on extra thick.

Midas named the boat *Icarus* because; well, because he was a little fuzzy on his Greek mythology.

At a gala press conference Midas

announced that for the *Icarus's* maiden

voyage he was inviting only the A-est of Woodland's A-List to join him, thereby guaranteeing (by his own admission), that it would be the most totally classy, star-studded event ever. Naturally, this news set off weeks of feverish publicity about and kissing up to Midas.

On the big day, as the select few who'd been selected walked up the red-carpeted gangplank, each was given a gift bag full of gold-plated goodies that included a 1/32"-scale model of the *Icarus*, an anchor-shaped keychain and a hefty jewelry box, all made with leftover iron from the ship's anchor and stuffed with gift certificates to swanky hotels, resorts, casinos, spas and restaurants that Midas owned a piece of.

Midas's current wife christened the boat by breaking a bottle of overpriced champagne over its bow.

Nobody noticed the crack it made.

The spectators on the dock cheered on cue as the *Icarus* pulled away and headed across Woodland's harbor, glistening in the sunlight as it sailed toward the open sea.

Just as it passed the lighthouse, however, the crack in its bow split wide open and water began rushing in.

Fortunately, everyone made it into the lifeboats before the *Icarus* went under. Unfortunately, the lifeboats were made just as badly as the rest of the ship and now, filled with swells refusing to let go of their swag, went down like a gift bag of hammers.

Some of the passengers got back to shore using their trophy wives as floatation devices but most went down with the ship.

Midas was among the survivors and at the inquest claimed the incident was an "Act of God," specifically, Neptune, god of the sea. Amazingly, this strategy worked and Midas was found not liable for the sinking and went on to produce and star as himself in two of the three movies made about the incident.

Last we heard he was buying a blimp.

Moral: *Not everything that glitters is gold, much less worth holding onto.*

The Six Blond Men & The Elephant

ONCE UPON A TIME six blond men came out of a movie theater still wearing their 3D glasses, got lost and wandered into a remote part of the Woodland.

As they stood in a clearing, trying to figure out where the parking valet might be, an elephant sauntered toward them.

"Whoa," they exclaimed, "It's as if it's coming right at us!"

When the elephant stopped in front of them (they were in its way), they circled around it, each of them now facing a different part of the animal.

The blond man standing at the elephant's side touched it and said,

"Well, special effect or not, it needs moisturizer!"

One blond man put his arms around the left rear leg and declared, "Oh! It's an umbrella stand; my great-grandmother had

one just like it!"

"Oh, crap!" said the blond man behind the elephant who'd just realized what he was standing in.

"It's really heavy," groaned the blond man the elephant had stepped on.

"This is so much better than just 2D," said the blond man at the front of the elephant and watching as it swung its trunk and flapped it ears.

"Maybe it's a metaphor for something," one of them asked.

While the others considered that possibility, the elephant's trainer, who they hadn't noticed riding on top of the beast, spoke up, "Would you guys please move out of the way, we've got a circus to get to."

The blond men were so startled they jumped back, clearing the path, and the elephant lumbered away slowly.

After it was gone, one of the blond men said, "You know, until it started talking, I was beginning to think it might actually be an elephant."

Moral: *Sometimes an elephant is just an elephant, no matter what it says.*